Books by ALMA FLOR ADA
THE GOLD COIN
MY NAME IS MARÍA ISABEL
SERAFINA'S BIRTHDAY
THE UNICORN OF THE WEST
WHERE THE FLAME TREES BLOOM
THE MALACHITE PALACE
UNDER THE ROYAL PALMS
THE THREE GOLDEN ORANGES

Books by LESLIE TRYON
ALBERT'S ALPHABET
ALBERT'S BALL GAME
ALBERT'S BIRTHDAY
ALBERT'S CHRISTMAS
ALBERT'S FIELD TRIP
ALBERT'S HALLOWEEN
ALBERT'S PLAY
ALBERT'S THANKSGIVING
ONE GAPING WIDE-MOUTHED HOPPING FROG
PATSY SAYS

Books by ALMA FLOR ADA
and illustrated by LESLIE TRYON
DEAR PETER RABBIT
YOURS TRULY, GOLDILOCKS

With Love, Little Red Hen

With Love,

ALMA FLOR ADA

Little Red Hen

illustrated by
LESLIE TRYON

ATHENEUM BOOKS for YOUNG READERS
New York London Toronto Sydney New Delhi

To my wonderful seven:
Timothy Paul, Samantha Rose,
Camila Rosa, Daniel Antonio,
Victoria Anne, Cristina Isabel,
Jessica Emilia, with all my love
—A. F. A.

For the dear Good lady, Dorothy, with love
—L. T.

Atheneum Books for Young Readers
An imprint of Simon & Schuster Children's Publishing Division
1230 Avenue of the Americas
New York, New York 10020

Text copyright © 2001 by Alma Flor Ada
Illustrations copyright © 2001 by Leslie Tryon
Also available in an Atheneum Books for Young Readers hardcover edition.
Book design by Michael Nelson
The illustrations were rendered in pen-and-ink with watercolor.
Manufactured in China
14 15 16 17 18 19 20

Library of Congress Cataloging-in-Publication Data
Ada, Alma Flor.
With love, little red hen / written by Alma Flor Ada ;
illustrated by Leslie Tryon. —1st ed.
p.   cm.
Summary: A series of letters describe the actions of Goldilocks, Peter
Rabbit, the Three Pigs, Little Red Hen, and other storybook characters
when Little Red Hen and her chicks become the target of
the unsavory Wolf and his cousin, Fer O'Cious.
ISBN 978-0-689-82581-1 (hc)
[1. Characters in literature—Fiction.
2. Letters—Fiction.]
I. Tryon, Leslie, ill. II. Title.
PZ7.A44445 Paao 2001
[E]—dc21   00-042021
ISBN 978-0-689-87061-3 (pbk)
0616 SCP

Avenue of the Elms
Happy Valley
May 21

Hetty Henny
Forest Drive
Hidden Meadow

Dear cousin Hetty,

   Happy Valley is a beautiful place, and I am pleased to have found a nice little cottage. I look forward to raising my chicks where there is so much space for them to run and play.

   I must confess, though, that I'm a little bit disappointed by our neighbors, Mr. Dog, Mr. Goose, and Mr. Cat. They are not very neighborly. When I asked if they could help me clear the field behind the house to plant corn, they each answered, "Not I"; "Not I"; "Not I." So I have done all the plowing myself.

   My seven chicks are too little to help me with such hard work, but they kept me company and cheered me up.

   Now I'm going to give the chicks their dinner, tuck them in bed, and read them their favorite book.

   Please write soon. I would love to hear from you.

With Love,
   Little Red Hen

P. S. The chicks send you hugs and pecks.

Cardinal Cottage
Riding Lane
May 24

Goldilocks McGregor
McGregor's Farm
Veggie Lane

Dear Goldi,

Thank you for your letter about going to pick berries with Peter Rabbit and his sisters, Flopsy, Mopsy, and Cottontail. It sounds like so much fun! Have you been to their home yet? I would love to see Rabbit's Burrow.

I did not write back before because I spent two weeks at my grandma's house. I had a wonderful time. When we took walks, we made sure to stay on Royal Road. As you know, those awful wolves we encountered never come out to the main road.

During one of our walks, we saw that there is a new family living on Avenue of the Elms—a very busy hen with a bunch of her little chicks. She was tending to a field of newly sprouted corn all by herself and, although it seemed like very hard work, she was singing and her chicks were singing along, too. It was quite wonderful to watch.

I wanted to help, but Grandma did not think it proper. She thinks I was so taken by this hen because she is red, and everyone knows how much I like red. The truth is that she was working so hard and she really needed the help.

I hope I can see you soon.

Your friend,
Little Red Riding Hood

Forest Drive
Hidden Meadow
May 30

Ms. Red Hen
Avenue of the Elms
Happy Valley

Dearest cousin,

How wonderful to hear you have moved to Happy Valley at last. It is indeed a beautiful place to raise your young chicks. But I warn you not to let them go into the forest alone. Although I have never seen any, there is word around that there are some nasty creatures in the woods.

Your planting corn sounds exhausting, and you were wise to ask your neighbors to help. Maybe now that you have done the plowing and sowing, they will help out with the weeding and the other work a hearty, plentiful crop demands. Wouldn't that be nice?

Personally I keep very busy. I have recently painted my house all white. It looks so clean, it shines. I am now making new curtains and embroidering a tablecloth and napkins. It seems I am always with a sewing needle in my hand, and scissors, thread, and thimble in my pocket.

Let me hear how your corn works out. And let's get together soon!

Your loving cousin,

Hetty Hen

McGregor's Farm
Veggie Lane
June 3

Little Red Riding Hood
Cardinal Cottage
Riding Lane

Dear Little Red Riding Hood,

How do you always manage to see such unusual things? A red hen and her chicks singing while plowing a field! I would like to see that. I can assure you my father does not sing while he plows. He actually gets rather cross.

I have not yet been to Rabbit's Burrow. But, guess what? Mrs. Rabbit wants to invite us all to a picnic. She says she will never be able to thank Mother Bear enough for saving her son, Peter, from those wolves last spring, but that a picnic would be a "nice gesture." So one of your wishes will soon come true.

I have been thinking about that hen you saw. Why not be good neighbors and give her a hand? The days are pretty long now that it's getting toward summer, and I can get away after watering the lettuce. The hen is not planting carrots, so we won't have to worry about Peter getting distracted. The Three Pigs certainly should be strong enough. Shall I ask them? What about starting next Wednesday?

Your friend,

Goldilocks

P. S. Let's make this a surprise. What time does the hen go inside to put those chicks to bed?

Majestic Tower
Hidden Lane
Wooden Heights
June 15

Mr. Wolfy Lupus
Wolf Lane
Oakshire

Dear Wolfy,

Great news! Having finally recuperated from the disastrous attack of that angry Mother Bear, I reinitiated last week my surveillance of the woods. I have discovered that a new innocent morsel has just moved to the neighborhood.

Do not worry, our decision to keep away from pigs and rabbits stands firm! The new neighbor is an appetizing hen, not to mention her brood of chicks.

The poor creature has just finished planting a cornfield. We will wait until later in the summer, when the corn is ripe and she and her chicks have grown plump. Then we can feast on chicken and corn. I tried to enlist the help of some of her neighbors, to notify me when the corn is just ready to pick. I did not get far with a silly dog and a simple goose who seemed so startled by my presence, they could not utter a word. But I finally got through to one of her neighbors, a cat named Lazy Feline, I used to know in my smuggling days. He has promised to spy on her and let me know when the time is right. We can make more specific plans then!

Keep well,
Fer O'Cious

Wolf Lane
Oakshire
June 19

Mr. Fer O'Cious
Majestic Tower
Hidden Lane
Wooden Heights

Dear Cousin Fer,

Luck does seem to be finally coming our way! Yes, after our bungled confrontation last spring, we can say good-bye forever to rabbits and pigs—and their impertinent friends the Bears. As I passed that rabbit's house last Sunday, I saw them all enjoying a picnic. (You should have seen how the Mother Bear was watching over them all. As if I would have bothered with any of them!)

Now that you mention our seeking better prey, I remember a freshly painted white cottage on Forest Drive that I had not noticed before. It, too, is occupied by a hen who seems busy, busy, busy, working around her house. I for one wouldn't want so much work to wear her down or make her tough. I will catch her at the first opportunity. Of course, I'll let you know so you can share in the feast!

Until then,

Wolfy

Ms. Red Hen
Avenue of the Elms
Happy Valley

Dearest, dearest cousin Red,

Oh my, oh my, how lucky I am!

Yesterday I had the biggest scare of my life. I still can't believe I'm here, in my own little house, able to write to you about it.

It was such a hot day that I decided to find a cool place by the stream close to my house to do my sewing. As I was walking along the bank, looking for a shady tree, I was suddenly lifted in the air. I was unable to see a thing.

It took me several moments before I realized I had been stuffed inside an old sack. My captor was carrying me away, and I was so frightened, I could hardly breathe.

Fortunately, the fellow was either very lazy or out of shape, because he got tired and stopped to rest. He sat under a tree and fell asleep, clutching the bag with me inside. I was desperately thinking of ways to escape when I remembered the needle, thimble, thread, and scissors in my apron pocket. So as soon as I heard loud snores, I cut through the sack with the scissors, placed a big stone inside the sack, and sewed it back up. I barely looked at my captor, a big mean-looking wolf, and ran all the way home.

Now that I am cozily at home, I can't but wonder what the wolf's face looked like when he opened the sack! It's a pity I'll never know!

Love from your safe and happy cousin,

Hetty Hen

June 25

Fer O'Cious
Majestic Tower
Hidden Lane
Wooden Heights

COME IMMEDIATELY. HEN CAPTURED. LET'S PARTY
TONIGHT.

SHE'S A PLUMP, HEAVY ONE. SAVE YOUR APPETITE.

Wolfy

Goldilocks McGregor
McGregor's Farm
Veggie Lane

Dear Goldilocks,

Now that we have been working in this cornfield, I understand why your father says that the life of a farmer is hard. I can also understand his moods a little better.

My hands are full of blisters, and my back hurts. I only hope the cornfield thrives and the red hen and her chicks have enough corn to last them through the winter. It's the only thought that helps me keep going.

What do you think of putting a scarecrow in the field? Could you ask the pigs if they have any old clothes? I wouldn't want us to do all this work simply to feed a few mean crows.

I'm too sore to write more. See you at the cornfield in two days.

Love,

LITTLE RED RIDING HOOD

Avenue of the Elms
Happy Valley
July 25

Ms. Hetty Henny
Forest Drive
Hidden Meadow

Dear Hetty,

When I wake up every morning my first thought is always how grateful I am to be alive. Now I'm doubly grateful because you are also alive! What a chilling experience.

I must say Happy Valley is turning out to be a place full of mysteries. My corn is growing nicely, but it seems as if it were taking care of itself. The soil stays moist in spite of the heat, and everything stays so nicely weeded. What is most surprising is that a scarecrow appeared last Thursday in the middle of the field!

Certainly none of this is the doing of my lazy neighbors. I went to ask them, ready to thank them, but all they say is: "Not I"; "Not I"; "Not I." I must say that I am increasingly wary of a glitter in that Mr. Cat's eyes. I just found out from the mail carrier that the cat's last name is really Feline, although his mailbox clearly says Mr. Cat. Do you find that strange? The corn should be ready to be picked in two weeks. So why don't you spend that Sunday with us?

I have been collecting recipes for dishes from all over the world made with corn. It is amazing how many dishes there are.

Looking forward to your visit,
    Your cousin Red

P. S. I'm thinking of leaving an invitation to join us pinned to the scarecrow's coat for whoever put it there. What do you think?

Majestic Tower
Hidden Lane
Wooden Heights
August 19

Mr. Wolfy Lupus
Wolf Lane
Oakshire

Dear Wolfy,

I am sending this brief note via a swift courier. Even after your visit to the doctor, traveling may still be difficult for you but we must hurry if our plans are to succeed. That good-for-nothing Feline has failed me. He fell asleep on the job. Now he reports that the hen has already harvested the corn and is busily cooking. It looks as if she is expecting guests, too. We must get there before her guests arrive if we want our corn-and-hen supper!

It is time for our feast! Come fast.

Yours,
Fer

Rabbit's Burrow
Hollow Oak
August 22

Goldilocks McGregor
McGregor's Farm
Veggie Lane

Dear Goldilocks,

I'm not very fond of writing letters. But I wanted to write this one. I want to say what a great idea it was for us to help Ms. Red Hen.

As you know, I love to eat vegetables, but it is even more fun to eat something I helped grow. It was wonderful to get together with so many old and new friends. How relaxing and peaceful it was in spite of the commotion off in the woods, near Mr. Cat's house.

It is especially nice to know Ms. Red Hen will have all that corn for her and her chicks for the winter.

One feels much better during the winter when the pantry is full. My mother is already beginning to can things for the winter. She makes wonderful marmalades and jams. Would you like to go pick some blackberries?

Your good friend,

Peter Rabbit

P. S. Thanks to Little Red Riding Hood for telling you about Ms. Red. I like Little Red Riding Hood more each day!

HIDDEN FOREST DIRECTORY

THE BEARS
Bear House in the Woods
Hidden Meadow

TEDDY BEAR
Cuddling Tree
Woodsy Woods

TURKEY LURKEY, M.D.
Resident Physician
Cure-It-All Clinic
Ailments Road

HETTY HENNY
Forest Drive
Hidden Meadow

WOLFY LUPUS
Wolf Lane
Oakshire

GOLDILOCKS McGREGOR
McGregor's Farm
Veggie Lane

FER O'CIOUS
Majestic Tower
Hidden Lane
Wooden Heights

OSITO
Villa Alegre
Happy Valley

THE PIGS
Pig One, Pig Two, Pig Three
Brick House
Woodsy Woods

temporarily:
Pig One
Straw House
Woodsy Woods

Pig One & Pig Two
Stick House
Woodsy Woods

THE RABBIT FAMILY
Mopsy, Flopsy, Cottontail, Peter, and Mrs. Josephine Rabbit
Rabbit's Burrow
Hollow Oak Road

SPEEDY RACCOON, Furrier
Forest Drive
Hidden Forest

MS. RED HEN
Avenue of the Elms
Happy Valley

LITTLE RED RIDING HOOD
Cardinal Cottage
Riding Lane

GRANDMA ROSE REDDING
Cottage in the Woods
Hidden Forest